BRINGING THE RAIN TO KAPITI PLAIN

A Nandi Tale

BRINGING THE RAIN TO KAPITI PLAIN

retold by Verna Aardema / pictures by Beatriz Vidal

PUFFIN BOOKS

PUFFIN BOOKS
Published by the Penguin Group
Penguin Putnam Books for Young Readers, 345 Hudson Street, New York, New York 10014, U.S.A.
Penguin Books Ltd, 27 Wrights Lane, London W8 5TZ, England
Penguin Books Australia Ltd, Ringwood, Victoria, Australia
Penguin Books Canada Ltd, 10 Alcorn Avenue, Toronto, Ontario, Canada M4V 3B2
Penguin Books (N.Z.) Ltd, 182-190 Wairau Road, Auckland 10, New Zealand

Penguin Books Ltd, Registered Offices: Harmondsworth, Middlesex, England

First published by Dial Books for Young Readers, a division of Penguin Books USA Inc., 1981
First published by Puffin Books, 1983
50 49 48 47 46 45 44 43 42

Text copyright © 1981 by Verna Aardema
Pictures copyright © 1981 by Beatrice Vidal
All rights reserved

ISBN 0-14-054616-2
LIBRARY OF CONGRESS CATALOG CARD NUMBER: 80-25886

Printed in U.S.A.

For my librarian,
Bernice Houseward
V. A.

For my parents; for my teacher
B. V.

This is the great
   Kapiti Plain,
All fresh and green
   from the African rains—
A sea of grass for the
   ground birds to nest in,
And patches of shade for
   wild creatures to rest in;
With acacia trees for
   giraffes to browse on,
And grass for the herdsmen
   to pasture their cows on.

But one year the rains
   were so very belated,
That all of the big wild
   creatures migrated.
Then Ki-pat helped to end
   that terrible drought—
And this story tells
   how it all came about!

This is the cloud,
   all heavy with rain,
That shadowed the ground
   on Kapiti Plain.

This is the grass,
    all brown and dead,
That needed the rain
    from the cloud overhead—
The big, black cloud,
    all heavy with rain,
That shadowed the ground
    on Kapiti Plain.

These are the cows,
    all hungry and dry,
Who mooed for the rain
    to fall from the sky;
To green-up the grass,
    all brown and dead,
That needed the rain
    from the cloud overhead—
The big, black cloud,
    all heavy with rain,
That shadowed the ground
    on Kapiti Plain.

This is Ki-pat,
    who watched his herd
As he stood on one leg,
    like the big stork bird;
Ki-pat, whose cows
    were so hungry and dry,
They mooed for the rain
    to fall from the sky;
To green-up the grass,
    all brown and dead,
That needed the rain
    from the cloud overhead—
The big, black cloud,
    all heavy with rain,
That shadowed the ground
    on Kapiti Plain.

This is the eagle
    who dropped a feather,
A feather that helped
    to change the weather.
It fell near Ki-pat,
    who watched his herd
As he stood on one leg,
    like the big stork bird;
Ki-pat, whose cows
    were so hungry and dry,
They mooed for the rain
    to fall from the sky;
To green-up the grass,
    all brown and dead,
That needed the rain
    from the cloud overhead—
The big, black cloud,
    all heavy with rain,
That shadowed the ground
    on Kapiti Plain.

This is the arrow
    Ki-pat put together,
With a slender stick
    and an eagle feather;
From the eagle who happened
    to drop a feather,
A feather that helped
    to change the weather.

It fell near Ki-pat,
    who watched his herd
As he stood on one leg,
    like the big stork bird;
Ki-pat, whose cows
    were so hungry and dry,
They mooed for the rain
    to fall from the sky;
To green-up the grass,
    all brown and dead,
That needed the rain
    from the cloud overhead—
The big, black cloud,
    all heavy with rain,
That shadowed the ground
    on Kapiti Plain.

This is the bow,
  so long and strong,
And strung with a string,
  a leather thong;
A bow for the arrow
  Ki-pat put together,
With a slender stick
  and an eagle feather;
From the eagle who happened
  to drop a feather,
A feather that helped
  to change the weather.

It fell near Ki-pat,
    who watched his herd
As he stood on one leg,
    like the big stork bird;
Ki-pat, whose cows
    were so hungry and dry,
They mooed for the rain
    to fall from the sky;
To green-up the grass,
    all brown and dead,
That needed the rain
    from the cloud overhead—
The big, black cloud,
    all heavy with rain,
That shadowed the ground
    on Kapiti Plain.

This was the shot
that pierced the cloud
And loosed the rain
with thunder LOUD!
A shot from the bow,
so long and strong,
And strung with a string,
a leather thong;
A bow for the arrow
Ki-pat put together,
With a slender stick
and an eagle feather;
From the eagle who happened
to drop a feather,
A feather that helped
to change the weather.

It fell near Ki-pat,
   who watched his herd
As he stood on one leg,
   like the big stork bird;
Ki-pat, whose cows
   were so hungry and dry,
They mooed for the rain
   to fall from the sky;
To green-up the grass,
   all brown and dead,
That needed the rain
   from the cloud overhead—
The big, black cloud,
   all heavy with rain,
That shadowed the ground
   on Kapiti Plain.

So the grass grew green,
and the cattle fat!
And Ki-pat got a wife
and a little Ki-pat—

Who tends the cows now,
    and shoots down the rain,
When black clouds shadow
    Kapiti Plain.

About the Author

Verna Aardema is a highly acclaimed storyteller and the author of many books of African folktales. Her most recent book for Dial, *Who's in Rabbit's House?*, illustrated by Leo and Diane Dillon, was an American Library Association Notable Children's Book and a *School Library Journal* Best Book of the Year, 1977. *Why Mosquitoes Buzz in People's Ears*, also illustrated by the Dillons, was awarded the Caldecott Medal in 1976 and was chosen as an American Library Association Notable Children's Book, as was a third Aardema-Dillon collaboration, *Behind the Back of the Mountain*.

Ms. Aardema was born in New Era, Michigan, and received her degree in journalism from Michigan State University. She now lives in Muskegon, Michigan, with her husband, Dr. Joel Vugteveen.

About the Artist

Beatriz Vidal was born in Argentina and received her Bachelor of Arts from Córdoba University. She has studied art with Ilonka Karasz, and her illustrations have appeared on UNICEF cards and publications including *Vogue* and *Woman's Day*.

Ms. Vidal currently lives in New York City. This is her first children's book.

About the Tale

This tale was discovered in Kenya, Africa, more than seventy years ago by the famous anthropologist Sir Claud Hollis. Sir Claud camped near a Nandi village and learned the native language from two young boys. He learned riddles and proverbs from the Nandi children, and most of the folktales from the Chief Medicine Man. This tale reminded Sir Claud of a cumulative nursery rhyme he had loved as a boy in England, one also familiar to us—"The House That Jack Built." So he called the story "The Nandi House That Jack Built" and included it in his book *The Nandi: Their Language and Folklore*, published in 1909. Verna Aardema has brought the original story closer to the English nursery rhyme by putting in a cumulative refrain and giving the tale the rhythm of "The House That Jack Built."